Freemason
Prayer Book

Elijah Abner

iii

DEDICATION

This book is dedicated to the builders and safe keepers of the craft. May it bring light to your darkness, comfort to your troubled soul, and compassion to your weary heart while on your masonic journey. Let us keep the memories of our departed brethren in our hearts till we meet again in that Celestial   Lodge   above.   SMIB

CONTENTS

Know Thyself

Prayer of Thanks

Great Architect of the Universe, we come before you with humble hearts and grateful spirits, recognizing the blessings that you have bestowed upon us. We gather here today as brethren of the Masonic fraternity, joined by our commitment to brotherhood, charity, and truth.

As we prepare to partake in this meal, we give thanks for the abundance of nourishment that you have provided for us. We ask that you bless this food and sanctify it for our bodies, that we may be sustained and strengthened in our work and service.

We also ask that you bless the hands that have prepared this meal, that they may be guided by your wisdom and grace. May this time of fellowship and nourishment deepen our bonds of friendship and fraternity, and inspire us to continue in our pursuit of virtue and knowledge.

We pray for those who are in need, those who are suffering, and those who are less fortunate than we are. May we always be mindful of our duty to assist our fellow human beings and to make the world a better place.

Finally, we ask for your continued guidance and protection as we carry out our Masonic duties and strive to live up to the high ideals of our craft. May we always be faithful to our obligations and committed to the values of integrity, compassion, and service.

We offer this prayer to the Great Architect of the Universe, who has given us all that we have and all that we are. Amen.

Masonic Blessing for Fellowship and Nourishment

Great Architect of the Universe, we come before you today with hearts filled with gratitude and thanksgiving. We are gathered here as brethren of the Masonic fraternity, joined together by our commitment to brotherhood, charity, and truth.

As we prepare to partake in this meal, we ask for your blessings upon this food, that it may nourish our bodies and sustain us for the work that lies ahead. We thank you for the abundance of blessings that you have bestowed upon us, and we pray that we may always be mindful of those who are less fortunate than we are.

We also ask for your blessings upon our fellowship, that it may strengthen our bonds of brotherhood and deepen our understanding of one another. May our time together be filled with joy, laughter, and camaraderie, and may we always be united in our pursuit of virtue and knowledge.

As we enjoy this meal, we are reminded of the many blessings that you have provided for us. We are grateful for the abundance of food and drink, and we pray for those who are hungry or thirsty, that they may find sustenance and relief.

Finally, we ask for your continued guidance and protection as we carry out our Masonic duties and strive to live up to the high ideals of our craft. May we always be faithful to our obligations and committed to the values of integrity, compassion, and service.

We offer this prayer in the name of the Great Architect of the Universe, who has given us all that we have and all that we are. Amen.

Invocation of Divine Guidance

Great Architect of the Universe, we come before you with open hearts and minds, seeking your divine guidance and wisdom. We are gathered here today as brethren of the Masonic fraternity, united in our pursuit of truth, virtue, and enlightenment.

We ask that you bless us with your divine guidance, that we may be inspired to seek truth and justice in all that we do. May we always be mindful of our duties to our fellow human beings, and may we strive to make the world a better place through our words and actions.

We ask for your blessings upon our Masonic endeavors, that they may be guided by your wisdom and grace. May we always be faithful to our obligations, and may we carry out our duties with honor and integrity.

As we contemplate your divine presence, we are filled with a sense of awe and wonder. We are humbled by the vastness of your power and the depth of your love. We pray that you will continue to guide us on our journey, and that we may always be open to your will and direction.

Finally, we ask that you bless each and every one of us, and that you watch over us as we go about our daily lives. May we be protected from harm and danger, and may we find comfort and solace in your loving embrace.

We offer this prayer in the name of our Creator, who has given us all that we have and all that we are. Amen.

Prayer of Unity and Service

Great Architect of the Universe, we come before you with hearts filled with gratitude and humility, recognizing that all good things come from you. We are gathered here today as brethren of the Masonic fraternity, united in our pursuit of brotherhood, charity, and truth.

We ask for your blessings upon our fellowship, that it may be strengthened and deepened by the bonds of unity and service. May we be united in our commitment to serve our fellow human beings, and may we work together in harmony and cooperation to bring about positive change in the world.

We pray for those who are less fortunate than we are, and we ask that you give us the strength and courage to assist them in any way that we can. May we be mindful of the needs of others, and may we always be willing to lend a helping hand.

We ask for your blessings upon our Masonic endeavors, that they may be guided by your wisdom and grace. May we be inspired to seek truth and justice in all that we do, and may we be faithful to our obligations to our brethren and to society at large.

As we go about our daily lives, we ask that you watch

over us and protect us from harm and danger. May we find comfort and solace in your loving embrace, and may we be guided by your divine presence in all that we do. We offer this prayer in the name of the Great Architect of the Universe, who has given us all that we have and all that we are. Amen.

Benediction for Brotherhood and Charity

Great Architect of the Universe, we come before you today with humble hearts, grateful for the many blessings that you have bestowed upon us. We are gathered here as brethren of the Masonic fraternity, bound together by the ties of brotherhood and charity.

We ask for your blessings upon our Masonic brotherhood, that it may be strengthened and deepened by the bonds of love and mutual support. May we always be there for one another, offering a helping hand when needed and providing comfort and solace in times of trouble.

We ask for your blessings upon our Masonic charity, that it may be guided by your wisdom and grace. May we be inspired to serve our fellow human beings with compassion and generosity, and may our efforts bring comfort and relief to those who are suffering.

We pray for those who are less fortunate than we are, and we ask that you give us the strength and courage to assist them in any way that we can. May we be mindful of their needs and may we always be willing to give of ourselves to help them.

As we go forth from this place, we ask that you watch

over us and protect us from harm and danger. May we be guided by your divine presence in all that we do, and may we always be faithful to our obligations to our brethren and to society at large.

We offer this prayer in the name of the Great Architect, who has given us all that we have and all that we are. Amen.

Grace for Gathering and Communion

Great Architect of the Universe, we come before you with hearts filled with gratitude and thanksgiving for the many blessings that you have bestowed upon us. We are gathered here today as brethren of the Masonic fraternity, united in our pursuit of truth, virtue, and fellowship.

As we gather together in this place, we ask for your blessings upon our communion. May the bonds of brotherhood that unite us be strengthened and deepened as we share this meal together. May our hearts be filled with joy and thanksgiving as we break bread together and share in this time of fellowship.

We ask for your blessings upon this food, that it may nourish our bodies and refresh our souls. May we be mindful of those who go without food, and may we be inspired to serve them with compassion and generosity.

We ask for your blessings upon our Masonic endeavors, that they may be guided by your wisdom and grace. May we be faithful to our obligations to our brethren and to society at large, and may our efforts bring about positive change in the world.

As we partake of this meal, we ask that you bless us with your grace and mercy. May we be filled with your love and may our hearts be lifted up in worship and praise. May your presence be with us always, guiding us and strengthening us on our journey through life.

We offer this prayer in the name of the Great Architect of the Universe, who has given us all that we have and all that we are. Amen.

Thanksgiving Prayer for Lodge

Great Architect of the Universe, we come before you with hearts filled with gratitude and thanksgiving for the many blessings that you have bestowed upon us. We are gathered here today as brethren of the Masonic fraternity, united in our pursuit of brotherhood, charity, and truth.

We give thanks for the gift of life and for the many opportunities that you have given us to serve our fellow human beings. We are grateful for the blessings of health, family, and friends, and for the many joys and pleasures that enrich our lives.

We give thanks for the gift of Masonic brotherhood, which has brought us together as a community of men who share a common bond of fellowship and service. We are grateful for the support and encouragement that we receive from our brethren, and for the opportunity to work together for the betterment of our communities and the world at large.

We give thanks for the gift of charity, which inspires us to serve those who are less fortunate than we are. We are grateful for the opportunities to give of ourselves, to share our time, talents, and resources with those in need, and to make a positive difference in the lives of others.

As we celebrate this season of Thanksgiving, we ask that you continue to bless us with your grace and mercy. May our hearts be filled with gratitude and joy, and may we always be mindful of the blessings that you have bestowed upon us. We offer this prayer in the name of the Great Architect, who has given us all that we have and all that we are. Amen.

Invocation of Wisdom and Virtue

Great Architect of the Universe, we come before you today as Freemasons, seeking your guidance and wisdom as we continue on our journey of self-improvement and service to our fellow human beings.

We ask that you bless us with the gift of wisdom, that we may always seek the truth and discern what is right and just. May we be guided by the principles of morality and virtue, and may we always strive to live up to the highest standards of conduct and character.

We ask that you bless us with the gift of courage, that we may stand up for what is right, even when it is difficult or unpopular. May we be inspired to do what is good and just, and may we never falter in our commitment to uphold the values of Freemasonry.

We ask that you bless us with the gift of compassion, that we may serve our fellow human beings with kindness and generosity. May we be mindful of the needs of others, and may we be inspired to help those who are less fortunate than we are.

We ask that you bless us with the gift of humility, that we may always be open to learning and growing in knowledge and wisdom. May we never become complacent or arrogant, but always be willing to listen to the opinions of others and to seek new insights and understanding.

As we go forth from this place, we ask that you watch over us and protect us from harm and danger. May we be guided by your divine presence in all that we do, and may we always be faithful to our obligations to our brethren and to society at large.

We offer this prayer in the name of the Great Architect, who has given us all that we have and all that we are. Amen.

Prayer for Masonic Enlightenment and Understanding

Great Architect of the Universe, we come before you today as Masonic brethren, seeking your enlightenment and understanding as we journey together in the pursuit of truth and knowledge.

We ask that you bless us with the gift of understanding, that we may comprehend the mysteries of your creation and the nature of our existence. May we be inspired to seek out knowledge and wisdom, and may we be open to the insights and perspectives of others.

We ask that you bless us with the gift of clarity, that we may see the world with a clear and unclouded vision. May we be guided by the light of reason and the principles of morality, and may we always seek to do what is right and just.

We ask that you bless us with the gift of discernment, that we may recognize truth from falsehood and good from evil. May we be vigilant in our pursuit of knowledge and wisdom, and may we always be mindful of the influence of bias and prejudice.

We ask that you bless us with the gift of enlightenment, that we may come to a deeper understanding of the mysteries of your creation and the nature of our existence. May we be inspired to seek out the truth and to live our lives in accordance with the highest ideals of human conduct.

As we journey together in our pursuit of knowledge and understanding, we ask that you watch over us and guide us on our path. May we be faithful to our obligations to our brethren and to society at large, and may we always be mindful of the responsibilities that come with our Masonic membership.

We offer this prayer in the name of the Great Architect, who has given us all that we have and all that we are. Amen.

Blessing for Masonic Ritual and Brotherhood

Great Architect of the Universe, we come before you today as Masonic brethren, seeking your blessing as we gather together in fellowship and in the performance of our rituals.

We ask that you bless this gathering with your divine presence, that we may be guided by your wisdom and your grace. May we be united in our purpose and our commitment to the principles of Masonry, and may we always be mindful of the importance of our rituals in strengthening our bonds of brotherhood.

We ask that you bless our rituals with your sacred power, that they may serve as a means of deepening our understanding of the mysteries of your creation and the nature of our existence. May they be a source of inspiration and enlightenment, and may they guide us on our journey towards greater knowledge and understanding.

We ask that you bless our brotherhood with your love and your compassion, that we may be a source of support and encouragement to one another. May we be guided by the principles of charity and benevolence, and may we always be mindful of the needs of our brethren and of society at large.

As we go forth from this gathering, we ask that you watch over us and guide us on our path. May we be faithful to our obligations as Masons, and may we always strive to live up to the highest ideals of human conduct.

We offer this prayer in the name of our Great Architect, who has given us all that we have and all that we are. Amen.

Healing and Comfort for a Sick Brother

Great Architect of the Universe, we come before you today with heavy hearts, as we lift up in prayer our beloved brother who is sick and in need of your healing touch.

We ask that you bless our brother with your divine presence, that he may feel the warmth of your love and the comfort of your embrace. May you surround him with your healing light, and may your grace bring him the strength and the courage he needs to face his illness.

We ask that you guide the hands of the healers who are attending to our brother, that they may be instruments of your love and your compassion. May they be guided by your wisdom and your grace, and may they be blessed with the skills and the knowledge they need to bring about our brother's recovery.

We ask that you comfort our brother's family and friends, and give them the strength and the courage they need to support him during this difficult time. May they be comforted by the knowledge that you are with them, and that they are surrounded by the love and support of their Masonic brethren.

As we come together in prayer and in support of our

sick brother, we ask that you watch over us and guide us on our path. May we be faithful to our obligations to our brotherhood and to society at large, and may we always be mindful of the needs of those around us.

We offer this prayer in the name of the Great Architect, who has given us all that we have and all that we are. Amen.

Masonic Prayer for Strength and Courage in Times of Adversity

Great Architect of the Univers, we come before you today as Masonic brethren, seeking your strength and your courage as we face the challenges and adversities of life.

We ask that you bless us with the strength and the fortitude to face our difficulties with courage and determination. May we be guided by the principles of Masonry, and may we be inspired by the examples of our Masonic brethren who have faced adversity with grace and courage.

We ask that you bless us with the wisdom to know what is right and the courage to do what is necessary, even when it is difficult or unpopular. May we be steadfast in our commitment to the principles of truth, justice, and honor, and may we always strive to live up to the highest ideals of our fraternity.

We ask that you bless us with the support and the encouragement of our Masonic brethren, that we may draw strength from their companionship and their wisdom. May we be mindful of the importance of our brotherhood, and may we always be ready to offer our support and assistance to those who are in need.

As we go forth from this gathering, we ask that you watch over us and guide us on our path. May we be faithful to our obligations as Masons, and may we always be mindful of the needs of our brethren and of society at large.

We offer this prayer in the name of our the Great Architect, who has given us all that we have and all that we are. Amen.

Unity and Harmony Amongst Brethren

Great Architect of the Universe, we come before you today as Masonic brethren, seeking your blessing and your guidance as we strive to promote unity and harmony amongst ourselves.

We ask that you bless us with the wisdom and the humility to recognize the importance of unity and harmony in our Masonic brotherhood. May we be mindful of the diversity amongst us and yet united in our common purpose and principles.

We ask that you bless us with the strength and the determination to overcome any barriers that may hinder our unity and harmony. May we be guided by the principles of tolerance, respect, and understanding, and may we always be willing to listen to each other and to work towards common goals.

We ask that you bless us with the compassion and the empathy to support and encourage our Masonic brethren who are facing challenges and difficulties. May we be ready to offer our assistance and our understanding, and may we be mindful of the needs and well-being of our brethren.

As we go forth from this gathering, we ask that you

watch over us and guide us on our path. May we be faithful to our obligations as Masons, and may we always be mindful of the importance of unity and harmony in our brotherhood.

We offer this prayer in the name of our the Great Architect, who has given us all that we have and all that we are. Amen.

Masonic Prayer for Wisdom and Guidance in Decision Making

Great Architect of the Universe, we come before you today as Masonic brethren, seeking your guidance and your wisdom as we make decisions that affect our lives and the lives of others.

We ask that you bless us with the wisdom to discern what is right and the courage to act on it. May we be guided by the principles of truth, justice, and honor, and may we always strive to make decisions that reflect these principles.

We ask that you bless us with the insight to recognize the consequences of our decisions, both for ourselves and for those around us. May we be mindful of the impact that our decisions have on our Masonic brethren, on our families, and on our communities.

We ask that you bless us with the humility to seek the guidance and the counsel of others when we are faced with difficult decisions. May we be open to the advice and the perspective of our Masonic brethren, and may we be willing to learn from their experience and their wisdom.

As we go forth from this gathering, we ask that you watch over us and guide us on our path. May we be

faithful to our obligations as Masons, and may we always be mindful of the importance of wisdom and guidance in decision making.

We offer this prayer in the name of our the Great Architect, who has given us all that we have and all that we are. Amen.

Prayer for Masonic Fellowship and Brotherhood Across Borders

Great Architect of the Universe, we come before you today as Masonic brethren, seeking your blessing and your guidance as we strive to promote fellowship and brotherhood across borders.

We ask that you bless us with the wisdom and the understanding to recognize the importance of building bridges across borders. May we be mindful of the common humanity that binds us all together, and may we be willing to reach out to our Masonic brethren in other lands and to learn from their experiences and their traditions.

We ask that you bless us with the humility and the respect to honor the diversity amongst us. May we be mindful of the different cultural, social, and political contexts that shape our lives, and may we be willing to listen to and to learn from the perspectives of our Masonic brethren across borders.

We ask that you bless us with the compassion and the empathy to support and encourage our Masonic brethren in other lands who may face challenges and difficulties that are different from our own. May we be ready to offer our assistance and our understanding, and may we be mindful of the needs and well-being of our brethren across borders.

As we go forth from this gathering, we ask that you watch over us and guide us on our path. May we be faithful to our obligations as Masons, and may we always be mindful of the importance of fellowship and brotherhood across borders.

We offer this prayer in the name of the Great Architect, who has given us all that we have and all that we are. Amen.

Prayer for Peace and Understanding

Great Architect of the Universe, we come before you today as Masonic brethren, seeking your blessing and your guidance as we strive to promote peace and understanding.

We ask that you bless us with the wisdom and the understanding to recognize the importance of promoting peace and understanding amongst nations. May we be mindful of the suffering and the pain that war and conflict bring, and may we be committed to working towards a world where peace and understanding are the norm.

We ask that you bless us with the humility and the respect to honor the diversity amongst nations. May we be mindful of the different cultural, social, and political contexts that shape our lives, and may we be willing to listen to and to learn from the perspectives of nations different from our own.

We ask that you bless us with the compassion and the empathy to support and encourage those who work towards peace and understanding amongst nations. May we be ready to offer our assistance and our understanding, and may we be mindful of the needs and well-being of those who work towards peace and understanding.

As we go forth from this gathering, we ask that you watch over us and guide us on our path. May we be faithful to our obligations as Masons, and may we always be mindful of the importance of peace and understanding amongst nations.

We offer this prayer in the name of the Great Architect, who has given us all that we have and all that we are. Amen.

Masonic Charity and Generosity in Serving the Needy

Great Architect of the Universe we come before you today as Masonic brethren, seeking your blessing and your guidance as we strive to serve the needy and to promote charity and generosity.

We ask that you bless us with the wisdom and the understanding to recognize the importance of serving those in need. May we be mindful of the suffering and the struggles of those around us, and may we be committed to working towards a world where everyone has access to the basic necessities of life.

We ask that you bless us with the humility and the respect to honor the dignity of those we serve. May we be mindful of the different circumstances that shape their lives, and may we be willing to listen to and to learn from their experiences.

We ask that you bless us with the compassion and the empathy to serve others with love and kindness. May we be ready to offer our assistance and our understanding, and may we be mindful of the needs and well-being of those we serve.

As we go forth from this gathering, we ask that you watch over us and guide us on our path. May we be

faithful to our obligations as Masons, and may we always be mindful of the importance of charity and generosity in serving the needy.

We offer this prayer in the name of the Great Architect, who has given us all that we have and all that we are. Amen.

Prayer for Protection and Guidance in Times of Travel

Great Architect of the Universe, we come before you today as Masonic brethren, seeking your protection and guidance as we embark on our travels.

We ask that you bless us with the wisdom and the understanding to make good choices as we journey from place to place. May we be mindful of our surroundings and the needs of others, and may we be guided towards safe and fruitful travels.

We ask that you bless us with the strength and the courage to face any challenges that may come our way. May we be mindful of our Masonic obligations, and may we remain faithful to our principles and values as we journey forth.

We ask that you bless us with the compassion and the empathy to support and encourage one another as we travel. May we be mindful of the needs and well-being of our Masonic brethren, and may we be ready to offer our assistance and our understanding whenever needed.

As we go forth from this gathering, we ask that you watch over us and guide us on our path. May we be faithful to our obligations as Masons, and may we always be mindful of the importance of protection and guidance in times of travel.

We offer this prayer in the name of the Great Architect, who has given us all that we have and all that we are. Amen.

Prayer for Masonic Illumination and Enlightenment in Knowledge

Great Architect of the Universe, we come before you today as Masonic brethren, seeking your illumination and enlightenment as we seek knowledge and understanding.

We ask that you bless us with the wisdom and the understanding to seek knowledge with humility and respect. May we be mindful of the complexities of the world around us, and may we be guided by the principles of truth and virtue as we seek to expand our understanding.

We ask that you bless us with the curiosity and the determination to pursue knowledge with passion and commitment. May we be mindful of the power and the responsibility that comes with knowledge, and may we be committed to using it for the betterment of all.

We ask that you bless us with the clarity and the discernment to distinguish between truth and falsehood. May we be mindful of the dangers of ignorance and misinformation, and may we be guided by the light of truth as we seek to navigate the world around us.

As we go forth from this gathering, we ask that you watch over us and guide us on our path. May we be faithful to our obligations as Masons, and may we always be mindful of the importance of illumination and enlightenment in our pursuit of knowledge.

We offer this prayer in the name of the Great Architect, who has given us all that we have and all that we are. Amen.

Humility and Gratitude in Times of Success

Great Architect of the Universe, we come before you today as Masonic brethren, humbled by the blessings and successes that you have bestowed upon us.

We ask that you bless us with the humility and the gratitude to recognize that all that we have and all that we are comes from you. May we be mindful of the role that our Masonic principles and values have played in our success, and may we always remember to give thanks for the blessings that we have received.

We ask that you bless us with the generosity and the compassion to share our blessings with others. May we be mindful of the needs and struggles of our Masonic brethren and those around us, and may we be guided by the principles of charity and service as we seek to give back to our communities.

We ask that you bless us with the strength and the determination to use our success for the betterment of all. May we be mindful of the responsibilities that come with success, and may we be committed to using our resources and our influence for the greater good.

As we go forth from this gathering, we ask that you watch over us and guide us on our path. May we be

faithful to our obligations as Masons, and may we always be mindful of the importance of humility and gratitude in times of success.

We offer this prayer in the name of the Great Architect, who has given us all that we have and all that we are. Amen.

Reverence and Adoration for the Great Architect

Great Architect of the Universe, we come before you today as Masonic brethren, filled with reverence and adoration for your infinite wisdom, power, and love.

We ask that you bless us with the humility and the gratitude to recognize the beauty and the wonder of the world that you have created. May we be mindful of the complexities and mysteries of the universe, and may we be guided by the principles of reverence and awe as we seek to understand our place in it.

We ask that you bless us with the faith and the devotion to seek your will and your guidance in all that we do. May we be mindful of the importance of prayer and meditation in our Masonic journey, and may we be committed to cultivating a deeper relationship with you.

We ask that you bless us with the courage and the compassion to reflect your love and your light in the world around us. May we be mindful of the challenges and struggles that we face as Masons, and may we be guided by the principles of justice and mercy as we seek to make the world a better place.

As we go forth from this gathering, we ask that you watch over us and guide us on our path. May we be faithful to our obligations as Masons, and may we always be mindful of the importance of reverence and adoration for the Great Architect of the Universe.

We offer this prayer in the name of the Great Architect, who has given us all that we have and all that we are. Amen.

Prayer for Masonic Charity and Compassion towards the Needy

Great Architect of the Universe, as Masonic brethren, we come before you with humble hearts and a deep desire to serve those in need. We ask for your guidance and blessings as we seek to embody the principles of charity and compassion in our daily lives.

We recognize that there are many in our communities who are struggling, whether due to illness, poverty, or other challenges. We ask that you bless us with the wisdom and the resources to help those in need, and may we always be mindful of the importance of reaching out to those who are less fortunate than ourselves.

We ask that you bless us with the generosity and the compassion to share our blessings with others. May we be guided by the principles of mercy and kindness as we seek to make a positive impact in the lives of those around us.

We ask that you bless us with the courage and the commitment to make a difference in the world. May we be mindful of the importance of working together as a Masonic fraternity to address the challenges that face our communities, and may we always be guided by the principles of love and service.

As we go forth from this gathering, we ask for your continued blessings and guidance. May we always be mindful of the importance of charity and compassion towards the needy, and may we always be committed to making a positive difference in the world.

We offer this prayer in the name of the Great Architect, who has blessed us with so much and calls us to serve others. Amen.

Masonic Generosity and Kindness for those in Need

Great Architect of the Universe, we come before you as Masonic brethren with grateful hearts for the blessings that you have bestowed upon us. As we gather here today, we ask for your guidance and blessings as we seek to embody the principles of generosity and kindness towards the needy.

We recognize that there are many in our communities who are struggling, whether due to poverty, illness, or other challenges. We ask that you bless us with the resources and the compassion to help those in need, and may we always be mindful of the importance of giving back to our communities.

We ask that you bless us with the generosity and the kindness to share our blessings with others. May we be guided by the principles of charity and love as we seek to make a positive impact in the lives of those around us.

We ask that you bless us with the humility and the empathy to understand the needs of others. May we be mindful of the importance of listening to those who are less fortunate than ourselves, and may we always be committed to meeting their needs as best we can.

As we go forth from this gathering, we ask for your continued blessings and guidance. May we always be mindful of the importance of generosity and kindness towards the needy, and may we always be committed to making a positive difference in the world.

We offer this prayer in the name of the Great Architect, who has blessed us with so much and calls us to serve others. Amen.

Service and Compassion to Those in Need

Great Architect of the Universe, we gather as Masonic brethren, called to serve those in need with compassion and humility. We thank you for the blessings you have bestowed upon us and ask for your guidance as we seek to serve others in your name.

We pray for those who are suffering, whether they are struggling with illness, poverty, or other hardships. May we be filled with compassion and empathy as we seek to understand their struggles and extend a helping hand.

We ask for your blessings as we strive to make a positive difference in the lives of those in need. May we be guided by the principles of charity and love, and may we be committed to serving others selflessly and with joy.

We pray for the strength and wisdom to do your work. May we be filled with the courage to take action, the humility to learn from others, and the wisdom to discern where we can make the greatest impact.

We ask that you bless us with the resources we need to serve others, and with the courage to use these resources for the greater good. May we be good stewards of the gifts you have given us, and may we use them to help those who are struggling.

As we go forth from this gathering, may we be filled with a renewed sense of purpose and commitment to serving those in need. May we be instruments of your peace, and may our service and compassion bring hope and healing to those who need it most.

We offer this prayer in the name of the Great Architect, who calls us to serve others with love and compassion. Amen.

Masonic Prayer for Charity and Outreach

Great Architect of the Universe, we come before you as Masonic brethren, united in our desire to serve those in need with charity and compassion. We recognize that we have been blessed with many gifts, and we ask that you guide us as we seek to share these gifts with others.

We pray for those who are suffering and in need, whether they are struggling with poverty, illness, or other challenges. May we be filled with a spirit of generosity and kindness as we seek to reach out to them and offer them the support and care they need.

We ask that you bless our efforts to serve others,. May we be guided by the principles of charity and love, and may we be committed to serving others selflessly and with joy. May we be inspired to look beyond ourselves and to see the needs of others with compassion and empathy.

We pray for the strength and wisdom to make a positive difference in the lives of those in need. May we be filled with the courage to take action, the humility to learn from others, and the wisdom to discern where we can make the greatest impact.

We ask that you bless our outreach efforts. May we be able to connect with those in need and offer them the support and care they require. May we be able to offer hope and healing to those who are struggling, and may our efforts be a source of comfort and encouragement to those who need it most.

As we go forth from this gathering, may we be filled with a renewed sense of purpose and commitment to serving those in need. May we be instruments of your peace, and may our service and compassion bring hope and healing to those who need it most.

We offer this prayer in the name of the Great Architect, who calls us to serve others with love and compassion. Amen.

Benevolence and Care

Great Architect of The Universe

As we gather here today as Masonic brethren, we are reminded of the many blessings you have bestowed upon us. You have provided us with an abundance of resources and talents that we use to better our communities and to support our fellow human beings.

We come before you now with humble hearts, seeking your guidance and inspiration in our efforts to help those who are less fortunate. We ask that you bless us with the compassion, generosity, and kindness needed to provide for the needs of the needy.

Help us to remember that we are called to serve and care for those who are suffering and struggling in our communities. May we always be mindful of their needs and use our resources and talents to make a positive impact in their lives.

May we be guided by your wisdom and love as we seek to provide for those in need. Grant us the strength and courage to continue our efforts, even when faced with challenges and obstacles. And may our acts of charity and kindness serve as a testament to your boundless love and mercy.

We pray for your blessings upon our Masonic efforts to

provide for the needs of the needy. May our actions be a reflection of your love and may they bring comfort, hope, and healing to those who are hurting.

In your holy name we pray, Amen.

Masonic Giving and Empathy

Great Architect of the Universe

We come before you today as Masonic brethren, humbly seeking your guidance and wisdom as we strive to give to those in need. We are grateful for the many blessings you have bestowed upon us, and we ask that you help us use these blessings to show empathy and compassion towards those who are struggling.

We acknowledge that there are many people in our communities who are suffering from poverty, illness, and other hardships. We pray that you grant us the empathy and sensitivity needed to understand their needs and to respond with kindness and generosity.

May our giving be motivated by a desire to serve others and to alleviate their suffering. Help us to remember that true charity involves not only giving of our resources but also giving of our time, our love, and our empathy.

We pray that you bless our efforts to give to those in need, that they may bring comfort, hope, and healing to those who are hurting. May our actions serve as a testament to the love and compassion you have for all of your creation.

We ask for your guidance and wisdom as we seek to live out our Masonic values of charity and empathy. May we continue to grow in our understanding of the needs of those around us and may our efforts to give reflect your boundless love.

In your name we pray,

Amen.

Masonic Prayer for Outreach and Support

Great Architect of the Universe

We come before you today with heavy hearts, knowing that many of our fellow beings are in need. We ask for your guidance and wisdom as we seek to reach out and support those who are less fortunate.

As Masonic brethren, we are called to embody the values of compassion and empathy. We are called to be beacons of light in times of darkness and to extend our hand to those who are struggling. We pray that you grant us the strength and courage needed to live out these values.

May our outreach and support be guided by your love and wisdom. May we never forget that every human being is created in your image and deserves to be treated with dignity and respect. May our actions reflect this truth.

We pray for those who are suffering from poverty, illness, and other hardships. May they feel the warmth of your love and the comfort of your presence. May they know that they are not alone, and that we are here to support and uplift them.

We ask that you bless our efforts to reach out and support those in need. May our actions bring healing, hope, and peace to those who are hurting. May they know that they are valued and loved by you and by us.

In your holy name we pray,

Amen.

Masonic Altruism and Assistance

Great Architect of the Universe

We come before you today as Masonic brethren, called to be selfless in our service to others. We pray for the grace to live out this calling with joy and generosity, especially when it comes to those who are in need.

You have commanded us to love our neighbors as ourselves, and to care for the most vulnerable among us. We ask for the courage and compassion to put these commandments into action, even when it requires sacrifice on our part.

We pray for those who are struggling with poverty, illness, and other forms of adversity. May they feel the comfort of your love and the support of their fellow human beings. May they know that they are never alone, and that we stand with them in solidarity and compassion.

We ask that you guide us in our efforts to assist those in need. May our altruism be driven not by a desire for recognition or reward, but by a genuine desire to serve and uplift our fellow beings. May our actions be a reflection of your boundless love and compassion.

We also pray for the strength and perseverance needed to continue in our efforts, even when progress is slow or obstacles arise. May we never lose sight of the great potential for good that lies within us, and may we always strive to be agents of positive change in the world.

In your name we pray,

Amen.

Masonic Prayer for Love and Kindness

Great Architect of the Universe

We come before you today to pray for those who are in need. We ask that you bless us with the wisdom and compassion to reach out and offer our assistance to those who require it. We recognize that there are many among us who are struggling and are in need of our love, care, and support.

We ask for your guidance in our efforts to help those who are less fortunate than us. May we be filled with the spirit of generosity and kindness, and may we always be mindful of those who are in need. May our actions be guided by love and compassion, and may we always strive to make a positive difference in the lives of those around us.

We pray for the strength and resources to help those who are struggling, and we ask that you bless us with the courage to stand up for what is right and just. May we always remember that we are all part of a larger community, and may we work together to create a world that is filled with kindness, compassion, and love.

We offer our prayer in the name of Freemasonry, and in the name of all those who are committed to serving others. May our efforts be blessed with success, and may we always strive to make the world a better place for all. Amen.

Prayer for Masonic Empathy and Compassionate Service to Others

Great Architect of the Universe

We gather before you with humble hearts and a desire to serve our fellow humans. We pray for the strength and courage to be able to extend our hands to those in need and to offer them comfort and support in their times of distress.

Grant us the wisdom to identify the needs of the less fortunate and to provide them with the assistance they require. Help us to be mindful of those who are struggling in our communities and to offer them our love, kindness, and compassion.

May our efforts be guided by the principle of charity and the values of Freemasonry, that we may be true to our obligations and serve as a beacon of hope to all.

We ask for your blessings upon our charitable works and for the ability to make a meaningful difference in the lives of those we serve.

May we always be mindful of your loving grace and seek to emulate your example of generosity and selflessness. We offer this prayer in gratitude and hope, in the name of the Great Architect. Amen.

Masonic Prayer for Generosity and Mercy

Great Architect of the Universe

We come before you with heavy hearts, knowing that there are many of our fellow humans who are struggling to make ends meet, who are in need of basic necessities, who are struggling with illness or disabilities, or who are facing other challenges that make life difficult.

As Freemasons, we are taught to be charitable and to help those in need. We ask that you guide us in our efforts to provide for the less fortunate and to show mercy and kindness to all those who are struggling.

We pray for the strength and resources to make a meaningful difference in the lives of those we serve. May our giving be inspired by love and guided by wisdom. May our service be a reflection of the compassion and generosity that we have learned through our Masonic teachings.

We also pray for the wisdom and guidance to know how best to help those in need. May we be guided by your light to provide the right kind of support, whether it be financial assistance, emotional support, or spiritual guidance.

We ask for your blessings on all those who are in need,

that they may find comfort, hope, and healing in the midst of their struggles. May they be surrounded by love and support, and may they find the strength to persevere through difficult times.

We offer our prayers in the name of the Great Architect of the Universe, who has taught us the true meaning of charity and compassion.

Amen.

Prayer for Safe Travels After a Masonic Lodge Meeting

Great Architect of the Universe

We give you thanks for the fellowship we have shared at this Masonic lodge meeting. As we prepare to depart and make our way home, we ask for your protection and guidance on our travels.

Grant us safe journeys, free from harm and danger. May our travels be smooth and uneventful, and may we arrive at our destinations safely. We ask that you watch over us and keep us safe from accidents, harm, and all forms of evil.

May your angels surround us and protect us from all dangers, seen and unseen. As we depart from this place, we pray that you continue to bless our Masonic fraternity and guide us in all our endeavors.

We ask this in your holy name,

Amen.

Masonic Prayer for Protection on the Road

Great Architect of the Universe

As we prepare to depart from this sacred place, we ask for Your loving hand to guide and protect us as we make our way home. We thank You for the fellowship and camaraderie we have enjoyed with our Masonic brethren, and we pray that You continue to bless and watch over us on our journeys.

We ask for your divine protection over every vehicle represented here. Shield us from any harm, danger, or accident, and help us to arrive at our destinations safely. May the bonds of our brotherhood surround us and keep us from any trouble or distress.

We also ask for your guidance and wisdom on the road. Grant us patience and understanding as we navigate traffic, and help us to be mindful of the safety of others around us. May we be responsible and respectful drivers, always striving to make the roads a safer place for everyone.

We ask for your blessing and protection not only on this journey but on all of our travels. Keep us safe from harm, protect us from danger, and guide us with Your infinite wisdom and grace.

Amen.

Blessing for Safe Journey Home After Lodge Meeting

Great Architect of the Universe

As we prepare to leave this place and return to our homes and families, we ask for your continued blessings and protection on the roads ahead.

Grant us the wisdom to drive with care and attention, the patience to tolerate delays and obstacles, and the courage to remain calm and composed in the face of any challenges we may encounter.

May the light of our fellowship and the bonds of brotherhood that we have strengthened in this lodge meeting, guide us and provide us with comfort and reassurance as we make our way.

We ask that you watch over us, our families, and all those who travel with us on this journey. Keep us safe from harm and deliver us to our destinations with ease and without incident.

We offer our heartfelt thanks for your blessings and ask for your continued guidance and protection in all our travels.

Amen.

Prayer for Guidance on the Way Home

Great Architect of the Universe, we pray to you for guidance and protection as we prepare to leave this sacred place and return to our homes.

We ask for your divine guidance to lead us on the right path and keep us safe from harm. May your holy angels surround us and protect us from all danger and evil forces that may come our way.

Please bless our cars, trucks, and any other vehicles we may use as we travel back to our respective homes. Help us to drive carefully and mindfully, so that we may arrive safely and without incident.

We pray that you will bless our families and loved ones who are waiting for us at home. May they be filled with joy and happiness at our safe return, and may we find comfort in their warm embrace.

Thank you for your love and care, and for keeping us safe throughout our time together. We give you all the praise and honor, now and forever. Amen.

Invocation for Safe Passage After a Masonic Assembly

Great Architect of the Universe

As we leave this Masonic assembly, we ask for your protection and guidance on our journey home. Please watch over us and keep us safe from all harm and danger.

We ask that you bless the roads we travel and guide us through any potential obstacles or challenges. Give us the wisdom to make good decisions and the strength to stay alert and focused.

We also ask for your blessings upon our fellow brethren who are traveling tonight. May they reach their destinations safely and without incident.

We thank you for your constant presence in our lives and for the many blessings you bestow upon us. Please continue to watch over us and keep us safe always.

Amen.

Masonic Benediction for a Safe Return Home

Great Architect of the Universe, as we leave this sacred space and prepare to journey to our homes, we ask for Your divine protection and guidance on the road. We thank You for the safety and fellowship that we have experienced during our time together as Masonic brethren.

We pray that You will bless us with the clarity of mind and steady hands necessary to safely operate our vehicles. Watch over us and guide us as we travel, keeping us safe from all harm and danger. May our travels be free from accidents, delays, and obstacles, and may we arrive at our destinations safely.

As we part ways and return to our daily lives, we ask that You help us to continue to embody the principles of Masonry in our thoughts, words, and actions. May we always act with integrity, compassion, and brotherly love, bringing light and goodness to those around us.

We offer this prayer in the name of the Great Architect of the Universe, the Creator of all things. Amen.

Prayer for Traveling Mercies After a Lodge Meeting

Great Architect of the Universe

As we prepare to depart from this Masonic Lodge meeting, we ask for your divine protection and guidance on our journey home. Please watch over us and keep us safe from all harm and danger as we travel on the roads.

Grant us the wisdom and discernment to make the right decisions on the road, to stay alert and focused, and to avoid any distractions that may lead to accidents. May your loving hand guide us and lead us to our destination safely and without incident.

We ask that you also watch over our fellow Masonic brethren who are traveling home tonight. May they also be kept safe and protected from any harm or danger.

We give thanks to you for this time of fellowship and brotherhood, and we ask for your continued blessings upon our lives and our families. May we always remember the lessons learned here tonight and strive to live out the values of our Masonic fraternity.

In your name we pray, Amen.

Masonic Petition for a Secure Homeward Journey

Great Architect of the Universe,

As we conclude this Masonic assembly, we ask for your guidance and protection on our way home. Watch over us as we travel, whether it be by land, sea or air, and keep us safe from all harm and danger.

Grant us the wisdom to make good decisions on the road, and keep our minds and bodies alert to avoid accidents and mishaps. Guide us on the right path and help us to arrive safely at our destination.

May we be surrounded by your divine presence and feel your loving embrace, providing us with the strength and courage to overcome any obstacles we may face.

We ask all these things in your holy name.

Amen.

Blessing for a Safe Drive After a Masonic Gathering

Great Architect of the Universe

As we leave this Masonic gathering, we ask for your divine protection and guidance on our journey home. We pray for traveling mercies and for your watchful eye to be upon us as we navigate the roads.

Grant us the wisdom to make sound decisions and the discernment to avoid any danger that may lie ahead. Keep us safe from harm and protect us from accidents or any other unforeseen circumstances.

We ask that you be with us every step of the way and that you grant us a safe arrival at our destination. May your grace and love be with us as we go our separate ways.

In your holy name we pray,

Amen.

Prayer for a Watchful Eye on the Road Home

Great Architect of the Universe

We come before you with gratitude for the fellowship and wisdom we have shared during our Masonic gathering. As we prepare to depart and return to our homes, we ask for your watchful eye to be upon us.

Guide us on our journey, and protect us from all harm and danger that may befall us. Give us the wisdom to make the right decisions, and the strength to remain alert and vigilant on the road.

May your grace and love be with us as we travel, and may our fellowship with one another continue to grow stronger. We ask for your blessings to be upon our families and loved ones, that they may be kept safe and secure until our return.

In your holy name we pray,

Amen.

Masonic Invocation for a Protected Journey Home

Great Architect of the Universe,

As we prepare to depart from this sacred place, we humbly ask for Your divine protection and grace. Watch over us as we journey through the night,

Guide us with Your wisdom and shining light. Grant us the strength to avoid danger and harm, And keep us safe from all that would cause alarm. As we travel on this road, we pray for Your hand,

To lead us safely to our homes and loved ones. Bless us with Your mercy and loving care, And keep us always in Your steadfast care.

May Your presence be with us on this journey, And may Your love be our constant sanctuary. We give thanks for Your blessings and Your grace, And pray for Your protection in every time and place.

Amen.

Masonic Prayer for Generosity and Service to the Community

Great Architect of the Universe we come before you today seeking your blessings as we strive to serve our community with acts of kindness and generosity.

We are grateful for the opportunities you provide us to be of service to our fellow humans, to show compassion and care for those in need. We recognize that it is through our generosity that we can make a positive impact on our community and bring light into the lives of those who are struggling.

May we always be mindful of our duty as Masons to support and uplift our community. Grant us the strength and the resources to give freely and generously to those who are in need, and may our actions be a reflection of the love and compassion that you have shown us.

As we go about our daily lives, help us to be aware of those who may be struggling and in need of our assistance. May we be guided by your wisdom and compassion, and may we act with kindness and love in all that we do.

We pray that our charitable acts will bring joy and comfort to those we serve, and may they be a testament to the values of our fraternity. May we always be ready and willing to give of ourselves for the betterment of our community, and may our actions inspire others to do the same.

We ask this in your holy name, Amen.

Prayer for Masonic Benevolence and Outreach to the Community

Great Architect of the Universe, we humbly come before you with grateful hearts, seeking your guidance and blessing as we strive to serve the community in need. As Masons, we are called to live a life of charity and compassion, to help those who are less fortunate, and to make a positive difference in the world.

We pray for the strength to carry out this important mission, to be generous with our time, talents, and resources, and to be mindful of the needs of others. We ask that you give us the wisdom and understanding to discern where our efforts can make the most impact, and to always act with integrity and sincerity in our charitable works.

May we always remember the teachings of our Order, that we are all brothers and sisters, and that our duty to one another extends beyond the walls of our Lodge. May we be inspired by the example of our Masonic forefathers, who sought to make the world a better place through their acts of kindness and generosity.

Guide us, O Great Architect, as we seek to serve the community with open hearts and loving hands. May our charitable works bring comfort and relief to those in need, and may we always strive to be a shining light in a world that is too often filled with darkness.

We ask this in your name. Amen.

Masonic Prayer for Generosity and Compassion to Those in Need

Great Architect of the Universe, we come before you today with grateful hearts, thankful for the blessings that you have bestowed upon us. As Freemasons, we strive to live our lives according to your divine plan, and to follow the tenets of our Order in all that we do.

We are mindful of those in our community who are less fortunate than we are, and we pray that you would give us the strength and the resources to serve them with generosity and compassion. Help us to see the needs of others and to respond with kindness, always seeking to alleviate suffering and to bring hope to those who are in despair.

We ask that you would bless the charitable works of our Lodges and of our brethren, that they may be effective in meeting the needs of those they serve. May our giving be done with pure motives, free from selfishness or pride, and may it be a reflection of the love and grace that you have shown to us.

We pray that our charitable efforts would bear fruit, and that through them, many lives would be touched and transformed for the better. May we always be faithful stewards of the resources that you have entrusted to us, and may our giving be a testament to your goodness and grace.

We offer this prayer in your name. Amen.

Prayer for Masonic Service and Care for the Less Fortunate

Great Architect of the Universe, we come before you with hearts full of gratitude for the many blessings you have bestowed upon us. We are humbled by your abundant love and grace, and we recognize that all that we have comes from you.

As Freemasons, we are called to be beacons of light in our communities, spreading kindness, compassion, and generosity to all those in need. We ask for your guidance and wisdom as we strive to fulfill this noble duty.

We pray for the less fortunate in our communities, those who are struggling to make ends meet and provide for themselves and their families. May we be instruments of your love, reaching out to them with open hearts and helping hands.

We also ask for your blessings upon those who serve in charitable organizations, dedicating their time and resources to alleviate the suffering of others. May their efforts be fruitful and may they find strength and inspiration in the knowledge that they are doing your work in the world.

May we always be mindful of our duty to serve the greater good, and may we continue to emulate the example set by our Masonic forefathers, who sought to uplift and support those in need.

We offer this prayer in your holy and precious name. Amen.

Masonic Prayer for Charity and Support to the Needy

Great Architect of the Universe, we come to you with humble hearts and a desire to serve those in need. We ask for your guidance and wisdom as we seek to extend our charity and support to the less fortunate in our community.

We pray that you bless us with the resources and means to offer assistance to those who are struggling, whether it be through monetary donations, volunteering our time, or simply lending a listening ear.

May we approach our charitable endeavors with open hearts and minds, and may we be mindful of the dignity and worth of each individual we seek to serve.

Grant us the strength and compassion to follow in the footsteps of those who have come before us, who have given of themselves so generously to the betterment of humanity.

May our actions be a reflection of our Masonic values of brotherhood, compassion, and service to others. May our efforts bring light and hope to those in need, and may we be inspired to continue this important work for the betterment of all. Amen.

Prayer for Masonic Altruism and Empathy towards Those in Need

Great Architect of the Universe,

We come to you in prayer today, seeking your guidance and blessings as we strive to extend our charitable efforts to those in need within our community.

Grant us the strength and resources to continue our work, to provide comfort and assistance to those who are less fortunate. Help us to recognize and respond to the needs of those around us, and to do so with compassion, empathy, and kindness.

May we never lose sight of the importance of serving others, and may our efforts always be focused on bringing comfort, hope, and relief to those who are struggling.

We ask for your continued protection and blessings on our charitable endeavors, and may our work always be guided by the principles of brotherly love, relief, and truth.

Amen.

Masonic Benediction for Giving and Kindness to the Community

Great Architect of the Universe

We gather in this sacred space as members of the Masonic fraternity, united in our commitment to charity and service. As we reflect on our obligations to our fellow beings, we pray for your guidance and blessings in our efforts to serve the community.

Grant us the wisdom to discern the needs of those around us and the courage to act on our convictions. May we always remember that charity and generosity are at the heart of our Masonic principles, and that we have a duty to share our blessings with those who are less fortunate.

May our efforts to serve the community be fueled by love and kindness, and may we always act with humility and compassion. May our deeds be a reflection of your divine goodness, and may they inspire others to follow in our footsteps.

As we go forth from this place, may we be ever mindful of our duty to serve the community and to spread the light of Masonry to all those we encounter. May our giving and kindness bring hope and comfort to those in need, and may we always remember that it is in giving that we receive.

We ask for your blessings on our Masonic work, and for your protection and guidance as we strive to serve the community with charity and love. Amen.

Prayer for Masonic Philanthropy and Outreach to the Less Fortunate

Great Architect of the Universe, we come before you with hearts full of gratitude and minds open to your guidance. As Freemasons, we strive to embody the values of charity and service, and we ask for your blessing on our efforts to support and uplift our fellow human beings.

We know that there are many in our communities who are struggling, who are in need of basic necessities like food, shelter, and clothing. We also know that there are those who are facing more complex challenges, such as illness, addiction, or mental health issues. We ask that you help us to be a source of comfort, strength, and support to these individuals.

We pray for the wisdom to recognize the needs of our communities and the courage to respond to them with generosity and compassion. May we be mindful of the impact of our actions and seek to uplift and empower those we serve.

May our charity not be simply an act of pity or condescension, but rather an expression of love and solidarity with our fellow human beings. May our service be not just a duty, but a joy and a privilege.

We ask for your guidance and protection as we seek to fulfill our obligations as Freemasons, and we pray that our efforts to give to those in need may bring light and hope to those who are struggling. Amen.

Masonic Petition for Compassionate Service and Charity to Others

Great Architect of the Universe,

We come before you with grateful hearts and a desire to serve others in need. We humbly ask for your guidance and strength as we strive to be a beacon of light and hope to those who are less fortunate than ourselves.

Help us to embody the values of charity and compassion, and to be a source of support and comfort to those who are struggling. May we have the courage to give generously of our time, talents, and resources to help those in need, and may we always be mindful of the impact our actions can have on others.

Bless us with the wisdom to discern where our efforts can best be directed, and the humility to recognize that we are but instruments of your will. May our acts of philanthropy and outreach be a reflection of your boundless love and mercy, and may they inspire others to follow in our footsteps.

We ask this in the name of all that is good and just, Amen.

Prayer for Masonic Love and Generosity towards the Community

Great Architect of the Universe

We come before you with grateful hearts, recognizing the blessings you have bestowed upon us. As members of the Masonic community, we are reminded of our duty to serve and uplift those in need.

We ask for your guidance and strength as we strive to demonstrate your love through acts of generosity and charity towards our community. Help us to see the needs of those around us and to respond with compassion and kindness.

May we always be mindful of our responsibility to those who are less fortunate and be driven by a desire to make a positive impact in their lives. May we always give with open hearts and hands, knowing that every act of kindness can make a difference.

We pray for the resources to continue our charitable work, and for the wisdom to use them effectively. May our efforts be a reflection of your love and a source of hope and comfort to those we serve.

In your holy name we pray, Amen.

Masonic Prayer for Outreach and Assistance to Those in Need

Great Architect of the Universe,

We come before you with grateful hearts, recognizing the blessings you have bestowed upon us. We also acknowledge that there are those among us who are less fortunate and in need of our help. We pray that you give us the strength and the resources to assist them in their time of need.

We ask for your guidance in our efforts to reach out to those who are struggling. May we be filled with compassion and empathy as we seek to understand their challenges and provide the necessary support. Help us to be kind, patient, and generous in our efforts to serve.

May our charitable works bring hope, comfort, and relief to those in our community who are suffering. May our efforts to give back inspire others to do the same, creating a ripple effect of kindness and compassion throughout our society.

We ask for your protection and guidance as we carry out our mission of service. Keep us safe from harm and help us to always act with integrity and humility. May our actions reflect your teachings and your love for all of humanity.

We pray for the strength and the resources to continue our efforts to serve the community. May our work be a testament to the values of our Masonic Brotherhood and the principles of charity, compassion, and love.

We ask all these things in your name, Amen.

Masonic Prayer of Congratulations for a Newly Raised Brother

Great Architect of the Universe, we come before you today with grateful hearts and joyous spirits to celebrate the accomplishment of our brother on being raised to the sublime degree of Master Mason. We thank you for the wisdom and guidance that you have bestowed upon him throughout his journey, and for bringing him to this point of success.

We give thanks for the work and dedication that our brother has put forth to achieve this honor, and we ask that you continue to bless him with the strength and courage to carry on in his journey of self-improvement and service to others. May his new degree be a symbol of his commitment to the principles of our fraternity and a testament to his character and devotion to the Craft.

As he continues on his path, we pray that you guide him towards greater understanding and enlightenment, and that he may find joy and fulfillment in his service to others. We ask that you bless him with wisdom, compassion, and the spirit of brotherhood, that he may continue to inspire and uplift those around him.

We offer our heartfelt congratulations to our brother and we pray that he may continue to grow and flourish in his journey as a mason. Amen

Divine Blessings for a New Fellowcraft

Great Architect of the Universe

We come before you with grateful hearts on this joyous occasion. Our brother has been passed to the degree of Fellowcraft and with understanding and enlightenment, and we give thanks for your guidance that has brought him to this point.

As Freemasons, we are bound by the sacred principles of brotherhood, charity, and truth. We know that through our shared dedication to these ideals, we can strengthen our bonds with one another and uplift the world around us.

We ask for your blessings upon our Fellowcraft brother. May he continue to grow in wisdom and virtue, and may his actions always reflect the noble teachings of our order. May his heart be filled with the light of your love, and may his steps be guided by the wisdom of your plan.

We ask that you bless our lodge and all those who labor within its walls. May we always seek to do your will and to serve humanity with selfless devotion. May we be worthy ambassadors of your grace and may our labors be crowned with success. Amen

A Freemason's Prayer of Unity

Great Architect of the Universe

Creator of all that is good and just, we come to you with humble hearts seeking to illuminate the bonds of brotherhood that unite us. As Freemasons, we strive to exemplify the principles of truth, honor, and virtue, which guide us along our path of service and duty.

We gather together in the spirit of unity, understanding that it is through our collective efforts that we can make a positive impact on the world around us. We pray that You bless us with Your divine light, that we may be enlightened to see the value and beauty in our differences, and to recognize the common threads that connect us all as brothers.

We ask that You guide us towards mutual understanding, empathy, and respect, that we may be better able to serve each other and the world at large. May Your light shine upon us, illuminating the path towards true brotherhood, and helping us to embrace the power of our collective strength.

May we always remember the sacred bond that unites us as Freemasons, and may we work tirelessly towards the betterment of ourselves and all humanity. SAmen

A Freemason's Prayer for Guidance

Great Architect of the Universe, we come before You seeking guidance on our journey as Freemasons. We ask that you shine Your light upon us, illuminating our path and leading us towards greater understanding and enlightenment.

We know that the road ahead is not always easy, and that we may face obstacles and challenges along the way. But with your guidance and support, we can navigate even the most treacherous terrain and emerge stronger, wiser, and more devoted to the noble principles of our Order.

We pray for the wisdom to discern the right path, the courage to follow it, and the strength to persevere when the going gets tough. May we never lose sight of our purpose as Freemasons, and may we always be guided by the principles of brotherhood, charity, and truth.

We ask that you bless us with your divine protection and guidance, and may your light shine upon us always, leading us towards greater understanding and enlightenment. We offer this prayer in the name of all that is good and just. Amen.

The Strength of Truth: A Freemason's Prayer for Moral Upliftment

Great Architect of the Universe

Creator of all that is good and just, we come before you seeking the strength to uphold the principles of truth and integrity that guide us as Freemasons. We pray for the moral upliftment of our souls, that we may be strengthened by Your divine grace and guided by the wisdom of your truth.

We know that the world around us can be filled with falsehoods and deception, and that it is our duty as Freemasons to stand firm in our commitment to honesty, honor, and virtue. We pray for the courage to speak the truth, even in the face of opposition or adversity.

May your light shine upon us, illuminating the path towards righteousness and justice. May we be emboldened by your divine presence to act with integrity and honor, to stand up for what is right, and to work tirelessly towards the betterment of ourselves and all humanity.

We pray for the moral upliftment of our souls, that we may be purified by Your divine grace and strengthened by Your unwavering love. May we be guided always by the principles of brotherhood, charity, and truth, and may our actions reflect the noble teachings of our Order.

Amen.

The Compassionate Heart: A Freemason's Prayer for Charity and Service

Great Architect of the Universe, we come before you seeking the compassionate heart that is the hallmark of Freemasonry. We pray that you fill us with Your divine love, that we may be inspired to serve humanity with selfless devotion and boundless charity.

We know that the world around us can be filled with suffering and injustice, and that it is our duty as Freemasons to work towards the alleviation of this suffering and the promotion of greater harmony and peace. We pray for the strength to be a source of comfort and support to those in need, and for the wisdom to know how best to serve.

May your light shine upon us, illuminating the path towards greater compassion and charity. May we be inspired by your divine love to work tirelessly towards the betterment of ourselves and all humanity, to be agents of positive change in a world that so often seems dark and uncertain.

We pray for the courage to be a voice for the voiceless, to stand up for the marginalized and oppressed, and to work towards a more just and equitable world. May our actions reflect the noble teachings of our Order, and may we always be guided by the principles of brotherhood, charity, and truth.

We offer this prayer in the name of all that is good and just. Amen.

The Universal Bond

Great Architect of the Universe, we come before you seeking the universal bond that unites all humanity. As Freemasons, we know that this bond transcends all differences and unites us in a shared commitment to brotherhood, charity, and truth.

We pray for harmony, that the divisions and conflicts that plague our world may be replaced by a spirit of mutual understanding, cooperation, and compassion. May your divine light shine upon all nations and peoples, illuminating the path towards greater unity and peace.

We know that the road ahead will not be easy, and that we may face many challenges along the way. But with Your guidance and support, we are confident that we can work towards a better future for all humanity.

May our actions reflect the noble teachings of our Order, and may we always be guided by the principles of brotherhood, charity, and truth. May our efforts towards global harmony inspire others to do the same, and may we be blessed with the strength, wisdom, and perseverance to see this vision through to fruition.

We offer this prayer in the name of all that is good and just. Amen.

Finding Light in the Darkness

Great Architect of the Univerrse we come before you seeking guidance and strength in times of darkness and uncertainty. As Freemasons, we know that life is filled with challenges and obstacles, and that it is our duty to overcome them with grace and resilience.

We pray for the wisdom to see the light in the darkness, to find hope in the face of despair, and to remain steadfast in our faith even in the most difficult of times. May your divine light shine upon us, illuminating the path towards greater understanding and peace.

May we be inspired by the noble teachings of our Order, and may we always be guided by the principles of brotherhood, charity, and truth. May we have the courage to face our fears and the strength to overcome them, knowing that you are with us always.

We pray for all those who are struggling with challenges in their lives, that they may find the support and comfort they need to overcome their struggles and find hope in the face of adversity.

May your grace and love be with us always, and may we find comfort and solace in your presence. Amen.

Rising Above Adversity

Great Architect of the Universe, we come before you seeking the strength and resilience to rise above adversity and overcome the challenges that life presents. As Freemasons, we know that the path to greatness is not an easy one, and that we must face many obstacles along the way.

We pray for the courage and determination to face these challenges head-on, to persevere in the face of adversity, and to rise above the obstacles that seek to hold us back. May your divine light shine upon us, illuminating the path towards greater strength and resilience.

May we be inspired by the noble teachings of our Order, and may we always be guided by the principles of brotherhood, charity, and truth. May we have the wisdom to learn from our struggles, and the humility to seek help when we need it.

We pray for all those who are facing adversity in their lives, that they may find the strength and resilience to overcome their struggles and emerge stronger on the other side.

May your divine grace and love be with us always, and may we find comfort and solace in your presence. We offer this prayer in the name of all that is good and just. Amen.

The Path of Perseverance

Great Architect of the Universe, we come before you seeking the strength and perseverance to overcome the obstacles that stand in our way. As Freemasons, we know that the journey towards greatness is not an easy one, and that we must have the courage and determination to face our challenges head-on.

We pray for the strength and endurance to stay the course, even in the face of adversity. May Your divine light guide us along the path of perseverance, illuminating the way towards greater strength and resilience.

May we be inspired by the noble teachings of our Order, and may we always be guided by the principles of brotherhood, charity, and truth. May we have the wisdom to recognize the lessons that our struggles have to teach us, and the humility to seek help when we need it.

We pray for all those who are facing obstacles in their lives, that they may find the strength and perseverance to overcome their struggles and emerge stronger on the other side.

May your divine grace and love be with us always, and may we find comfort and solace in your presence. We offer this prayer in the name of all that is good and just. Amen.

Embracing Change

Great Architect of the Universe, we come before you seeking the courage and wisdom to embrace change in our lives. As Freemasons, we know that change is an inevitable part of life, and that we must have the adaptability and resilience to grow and evolve along with it.

We pray for the courage to let go of the past, and the willingness to embrace new opportunities and experiences. May your divine light guide us along the path of adaptation and growth, illuminating the way towards greater understanding and fulfillment.

May we be inspired by the noble teachings of our Order, and may we always be guided by the principles of brotherhood, charity, and truth. May we have the humility to learn from our mistakes, and the gratitude to appreciate the blessings of each new day.

We pray for all those who are facing changes in their lives, that they may find the strength and resilience to adapt and grow, and that they may discover new opportunities and blessings along the way.

May your divine grace and love be with us always, and may we find comfort and solace in Your presence. We offer this prayer in the name of all that is good and just. Amen.

A Freemason's Prayer for Wisdom in Times of Uncertainty

Great Architect of the Universe, we come before you seeking the wisdom and clarity to navigate the uncertain times in which we live. As Freemasons, we know that the world can be a confusing and tumultuous place, and that we must have the wisdom and discernment to make the right choices in the face of uncertainty.

We pray for the wisdom to see the truth, even when it is obscured by the noise and chaos of the world around us. May your divine light guide us along the path of wisdom, illuminating the way towards greater understanding and insight.

May we be inspired by the noble teachings of our Order, and may we always be guided by the principles of brotherhood, charity, and truth. May we have the humility to acknowledge our limitations, and the courage to seek knowledge and understanding from those who can help us.

We pray for all those who are facing uncertainty in their lives, that they may find the wisdom and clarity to make the right choices and move forward with confidence and grace.

May your divine grace and love be with us always, and may we find comfort and solace in your presence. We offer this prayer in the name of all that is good and just. Amen.

The Journey of Self-Discovery

Great Architect of the Universe, we come before you seeking the enlightenment and understanding that comes from a journey of self-discovery. As Freemasons, we know that the path towards greater understanding and insight begins with the courage to look within ourselves, and the willingness to embrace the challenges and opportunities that come our way.

We pray for the clarity and insight to see ourselves as we truly are, and the courage to confront the areas of our lives that need healing and growth. May your divine light guide us along the path of self-discovery, illuminating the way towards greater understanding and enlightenment.

May we be inspired by the noble teachings of our Order, and may we always be guided by the principles of brotherhood, charity, and truth. May we have the humility to acknowledge our imperfections, and the determination to strive for greater excellence in all that we do.

We pray for all those who are on their own journey of self-discovery, that they may find the courage and strength to face their challenges with grace and wisdom, and that they may discover the beauty and wonder that lies within themselves.

May your divine grace and love be with us always, and may we find comfort and solace in your presence. We offer this prayer in the name of all that is good and just. Amen.

The Power of Forgiveness

Great Architect of the Universe, we come before you seeking the power of forgiveness, knowing that it holds the key to healing and renewal. As Freemasons, we know that forgiveness is a noble and powerful force that can transform our lives and the lives of those around us.

We pray for the strength and courage to forgive those who have wronged us, and the humility to seek forgiveness from those whom we have wronged. May your divine light shine upon us, illuminating the path towards forgiveness and healing.

May we be inspired by the noble teachings of our Order, and may we always be guided by the principles of brotherhood, charity, and truth. May we have the compassion to see the humanity in all those we encounter, and the grace to extend forgiveness even in the face of great adversity.

We pray for all those who are seeking forgiveness in their lives, that they may find the courage and strength to seek redemption and renewal. May your divine love and mercy wash over them, bringing healing and restoration to their souls.

May your divine grace and love be with us always, and may we find comfort and solace in your presence. We offer this prayer in the name of all that is good and just. Amen.

The Gift of Gratitude

Great Architect of the Universe, we come before you today with grateful hearts, seeking to express our appreciation for the many blessings that fill our lives. As Freemasons, we know that the gift of gratitude is a powerful force that can transform our lives and the lives of those around us.

We give thanks for the many blessings that we have received, both great and small, and for the countless ways in which You have touched our lives. May your divine light shine upon us, illuminating the path towards greater gratitude and appreciation for all that we have been given.

May we be inspired by the noble teachings of our Order, and may we always be guided by the principles of brotherhood, charity, and truth. May we have the humility to acknowledge the many gifts that have been bestowed upon us, and the generosity to share these gifts with others.

We pray for all those who are struggling to find gratitude in their lives, that they may be touched by your divine grace and love, and that they may find peace and contentment in the midst of their struggles.

May your divine grace and love be with us always, and may we find comfort and solace in your presence. We offer this prayer in the name of all that is good and just. Amen.

The Courage to Serve

Great Architect of the Universe, we come before you seeking the courage and strength to serve others with charity and generosity. As Freemasons, we know that the path of service is a noble and honorable one, and we seek to follow it with all our hearts.

We pray for the courage to put the needs of others before our own, and the generosity to give of ourselves freely and without reservation. May Your divine light shine upon us, illuminating the path towards greater service and charity.

May we be inspired by the noble teachings of our Order, and may we always be guided by the principles of brotherhood, charity, and truth. May we have the compassion to see the needs of those around us, and the courage to act on their behalf.

We pray for all those who are suffering in this world, that they may find comfort and solace in Your divine love and mercy. May we be the instruments of Your compassion and love, reaching out to those in need with open hearts and willing hands.

May your divine grace and love be with us always, and may we find comfort and solace in your presence. Amen.

Prayer for Unity in Diversity

Great Architect of the Universe, we come before You today seeking unity in the midst of diversity. As Freemasons, we know that the bond of brotherhood extends beyond our differences, and we seek to embrace this truth with open hearts and minds.

We pray for the wisdom to see beyond the surface differences that divide us, and the courage to embrace the unique gifts and perspectives that each individual brings to the table. May your divine light shine upon us, illuminating the path towards greater unity and understanding.

May we be inspired by the noble teachings of our Order, and may we always be guided by the principles of brotherhood, charity, and truth. May we have the humility to acknowledge our own limitations and biases, and the openness to learn from those who are different from us.

We pray for all those who are marginalized and oppressed, that they may find justice and equality in a world that often discriminates and divides. May we be the instruments of Your love and mercy, working towards greater unity and understanding in all that we do.

May your divine grace and love be with us always, and may we find comfort and solace in your presence. Amen.

The Mysteries of the Universe

Great Architect of the Universe, we come before you today seeking the contemplation and wonder that comes with the mysteries of the universe. As Freemasons, we know that the search for truth and knowledge is a never-ending journey, and we seek to embrace this journey with open hearts and minds.

We pray for the wisdom to understand the mysteries of the universe, and the humility to acknowledge our own limitations in the face of such wonder. May your divine light shine upon us, illuminating the path towards greater understanding and enlightenment.

May we be inspired by the noble teachings of our Order, and may we always be guided by the principles of brotherhood, charity, and truth. May we have the curiosity to explore the mysteries of the universe, and the courage to embrace the truths that we discover.

We pray for all those who are searching for truth and meaning in this world, that they may find comfort and solace in Your divine love and guidance. May we be the instruments of Your love and mercy, working towards greater understanding and enlightenment in all that we do.

May your divine grace and love be with us always, and may we find comfort and solace in Your presence. We offer this prayer in the name of all that is good and just. Amen.

Brotherly Love

Great Architect of the Universe, we come before you today seeking to honor the principle of brotherly love that is at the heart of our Masonic Order. We know that the bond of brotherhood extends beyond our differences, and we seek to embrace this truth with open hearts and minds.

We pray for the wisdom to see beyond the surface differences that divide us, and the courage to embrace the unique gifts and perspectives that each individual brings to the table. May your divine light shine upon us, illuminating the path towards greater unity and understanding.

May we be inspired by the noble teachings of our Order, and may we always be guided by the principles of brotherhood, charity, and truth. May we have the compassion to see the needs of our brothers and sisters, and the generosity to help them in their time of need.

We pray for all those who are in need of brotherly love, that they may find comfort and solace in the bond of brotherhood that we share. May we be the instruments of your love and mercy, working towards greater brotherhood and harmony in all that we do.

May your divine grace and love be with us always, and may we find comfort and solace in Your presence. We offer this prayer in the name of all that is good and just. Amen.

A Perfect Ashlar

Great Architect of the Universe, we come before you today seeking to honor the symbol of the perfect ashlar, which represents the ideals of perfection and wholeness that we strive towards as Masons.

We pray for the wisdom to recognize the areas of our lives that require improvement, and the strength to work towards achieving our highest potential. May Your divine light shine upon us, illuminating the path towards greater spiritual growth and personal development.

May we be inspired by the noble teachings of our Order, and may we always be guided by the principles of brotherhood, charity, and truth. May we have the diligence to work towards perfection in all aspects of our lives, and the humility to recognize that we are but mere mortals on a never-ending journey towards self-improvement.

We pray for all those who are seeking to perfect their own ashlar, that they may find the strength and courage to pursue their goals and aspirations with a steadfast determination. May we be the instruments of Your love and mercy, working towards greater unity and harmony in all that we do.

May your divine grace and love be with us always, and may we find comfort and solace in your presence. We offer this prayer in the name of all that is good and just. Amen.

Faith, Hope, and Charity

Great Architect of the Universe, we come before you today with hearts full of faith, hope, and charity. These virtues are the foundation of our Masonic brotherhood, and we seek to embody them in all that we do.

We pray for the strength to hold fast to our faith, even in times of trial and tribulation. May we find comfort in your divine presence, and may our faith be a source of inspiration and guidance in all that we do.

We pray for the hope that sustains us, even in the darkest of times. May we never lose sight of the light that shines within us, and may our hope inspire us to work towards a better tomorrow.

We pray for charity, the greatest of all virtues. May we always be mindful of those in need, and may we be instruments of your love and compassion in the world. May our charity be a testament to the bond of brotherhood that unites us as Masons.

Great Architect of the Universe give us strength and wisdom as we continue on our journey towards greater enlightenment, may these three virtues guide us always in our early travels. May our faith, hope, and charity be a beacon of light for all who seek truth and goodness in the world. Amen.

Making Good Men Better

Great Architect of the Universe, we humbly come before You today, seeking your guidance and wisdom as we strive to make good men better.

We are masons, bound together by a common purpose and a shared commitment to live our lives according to the principles of truth, morality, and virtue. We seek to become better men, not only for ourselves but for the betterment of all those around us.

We pray that You will give us the strength to face the challenges of life with grace and dignity, and the wisdom to discern what is right and just in all that we do. May we always strive for excellence in all aspects of our lives, and may we be role models for others to follow.

Help us to be patient and compassionate with ourselves and with others, recognizing that true growth and improvement takes time and effort. May we be willing to learn from our mistakes and to embrace new opportunities for growth and self-improvement.

Above all, we ask that you continue to bless our brotherhood, and guide us on our journey towards becoming the best versions of ourselves. May we always strive to make good men better, and may we be a shining example of the power of brotherhood and fellowship in a world that sorely needs it.

We offer this prayer in the name of all that is good and just. Amen.

Brother in Need

Great Architect of the Universe, we come before You today with heavy hearts, seeking your guidance and wisdom as we endeavor to help a brother in need.

We are bound together by the sacred bonds of brotherhood and fellowship, and we are called upon to support and uplift one another in times of trial and tribulation.

We pray that you will bless us with the strength, compassion, and resources needed to aid our brother in his time of need. May we be a source of comfort, encouragement, and hope to him, as we work together to help him through his struggles.

May we always remember the importance of our duty to one another, and may we never hesitate to offer a helping hand to those who are in need. May we be guided by the principles of charity and compassion, and may we always be mindful of our obligation to support our brethren in their time of need.

We offer this prayer in the name of all that is good and just, and we ask for Your blessings upon our brotherhood and all those who are in need of our support and compassion. Amen.

Distressed Brother

Great Architect of the Universe, we come before You today with heavy hearts, seeking your guidance and comfort for our brother who is going through difficult times.

We ask that you grant him strength and courage to face his challenges, and the wisdom to find the right path forward. May he find comfort in the love and support of his brethren, and may he feel the warmth of your divine light shining upon him, guiding him through the darkness.

We pray that you will surround him with your love and grace, and that you will give him the strength to persevere through this difficult time. May he be reminded that he is not alone, and that his brothers are here to support him every step of the way.

As we lift up our brother in prayer, we also lift up our hearts in gratitude for the blessings that we have received. May we always be mindful of our duty to support and uplift one another, and may we be guided by the principles of brotherhood, charity, and love.

We offer this prayer in the name of all that is good and just, and ask for your blessings upon our brother and all those who are going through difficult times. Amen.

A Freemason's Prayer for Overcoming Adversity

Great Architect of the Universe, we come before you in prayer seeking your guidance and strength as we face the challenges of life. We know that adversity is an inevitable part of our journey, but we also know that through your divine grace and the teachings of our fraternity, we can overcome any obstacle and emerge stronger and wiser.

Grant us the wisdom to discern the lessons that adversity brings, the courage to face our fears and doubts, and the faith to trust in your plan for us. Help us to remember that every setback is an opportunity for growth, and that every trial can be a stepping stone to greater heights.

We pray for our brethren who are currently facing adversity, whether it be illness, loss, or any other form of hardship. May they find comfort in the support of their fellow Masons, and may they draw strength from the teachings of our Craft.

Finally, we ask for your blessings upon our fraternity, that we may continue to be a beacon of light in a world often filled with darkness. May we embody the virtues of brotherly love, relief, and truth, and may we always strive to serve our fellow men and women with humility and compassion. These things we ask in your name. Amen.

The Imperfect Builder's Prayer: Striving for Perfection in a World of Imperfections

Great Architect of the Universe

As we gather in the spirit of brotherhood, we humbly acknowledge that we are imperfect builders in a world full of imperfections. We strive for perfection, but we know that we will never achieve it. Our work is like an unfinished ashlar, always in need of refinement and improvement.

Yet, we do not lose heart. We know that the pursuit of perfection is not a futile endeavor, but rather a noble one that can bring out the best in us. It is in striving for perfection that we become better men, better builders, and better servants to others.

Help us to embrace our imperfections and to use them as stepping stones towards our ideal selves. May we be patient and diligent in our work, always seeking to learn and grow. And when we stumble and fall, as we inevitably will, may we have the courage to pick ourselves up and continue on our journey.

May the imperfect ashlar of our lives be transformed into a thing of beauty and a source of inspiration for all who behold it. And may we, through our humble efforts, contribute to the building of a better world and be a shining light for all to see. Give us strength on our journey and light to know the way. This we ask in your name. Amen

Learning and Spreading Brotherly Love on Life's Journey

Great Architect of the Universe

As we journey through life, we recognize that our true mission is to spread brotherly love to all. We understand that this is not always an easy task, but one that is essential for our own growth and for the betterment of the world around us.

We recognize that we are all travelers on the journey of life, each with our own unique path and purpose. We are here to learn, to grow, and to contribute to the world around us. And as we journey, we are called to spread brotherly love to all those we meet, regardless of their background, beliefs, or circumstances.

We understand that spreading brotherly love is not just a matter of words, but of actions. It is about being kind, compassionate, and generous towards others, even when it is difficult. It is about treating others as we would like to be treated, with respect, dignity, and empathy.

As we travel on our journey, we ask for your guidance and wisdom. Help us to be open to new experiences, to learn from our mistakes, and to grow in our understanding of ourselves and the world around us. Help us to be instruments of your love, spreading kindness, generosity, and compassion wherever we go.

May we never forget that we are all brothers, united by a common bond of humanity. And may we always strive to treat others with the love and respect that they deserve.

So we ask for your blessings and guidance as we

journey through life. Help us to be lifelong learners, always seeking to grow in wisdom, knowledge, and understanding. And may we be faithful ambassadors of your love, spreading brotherly love to all those we meet.